GUMDROP
AND THE MONSTER

Story and pictures by Val Biro

PUFFIN BOOKS

'This is the life!' said Mr Josiah Oldcastle cheerfully. He was on holiday in Scotland, which was fine; the August sun was warm on his back, which was even better; and he was driving his vintage car Gumdrop, which was best of all.

'What's more,' he said to his dog Horace, 'I shall take lots of photographs. And you never know, I may even get one of the Loch Ness Monster herself, if there is such a thing!'

Which was all well and good, except that nobody had ever
taken a good one of the Monster yet. No wonder that Horace
gave a dubious 'woof'.

First they went to Edinburgh.
It was Festival time and the city
was crowded. There were so
many visitors round Gumdrop
that Mr Oldcastle could
hardly get out to take his
pictures. So he photographed
the visitors instead, with bits
of Edinburgh sticking out
behind them.

On the way to Loch Ness the road was blocked by a huge lorry.
There were three men standing beside it, wearing kilts and plaids.
'Ah, some real Scotsmen at last!' said Mr Oldcastle and promptly
took their photograph.
'Stop taking them there pitchers!'
shouted the biggest one, McBurp.
He hated being photographed.
'Move that old crock outer 'ere!'
snarled the middle one, McLurk.
He had no feeling for vintage cars.
'Git this darned dawg off of me!'
shrieked the smallest one, McSneak.
He was being attacked by Horace.

The men were so rude that Mr Oldcastle decided to drive on.
Anyway, he thought, their Scottish accents sounded most peculiar!

When they arrived at Loch Ness they found a lot of photographers there already. 'You are just in time,' said one of them, Professor Cyrus B. Whoppertaker of America. 'We were told for sure that the Monster would appear tomorrow morning!'

Another one called Watt A. Pitcher of the Sunday Pix said that the papers would pay thousands of pounds for a good photograph.

But Mr Oldcastle preferred to be on his own and drove along the
Loch to find a quiet spot.
He kept looking out over the water
and wondered if there really was a
monster there?
He should have kept his eyes
on the road instead, because
suddenly a huge lorry came
roaring towards him!

He braked hard, Gumdrop skidded, slipped off the road, slid down
the bank and lurched into the Loch. SPLASH!

Mr Oldcastle and Horace managed to scramble back to dry land, but poor old Gumdrop remained half-submerged.

'Serves you jolly right!' snarled the driver of the lorry, who was none other than McBurp.

'You can git that banger out yerself!' jeered McLurk.

'And do it, pronto,' warned McSneak, ''cos we need this spot for some'ink speshul tomorrer!'

And off they drove in a cloud of dust.

Mr Oldcastle tried and tried to pull
Gumdrop out, but it was no good.
It was getting dark by now and
there was nobody around.
'We shall just have to wait until
morning,' he told Horace, and
they settled down as best they
could and went to sleep.

Suddenly in the middle
of the night Horace
barked and Mr Oldcastle
woke up with a start. Was he
dreaming still? For there was
Gumdrop, slowly going UP the bank
and settling safely on the road again!
Mr Oldcastle rubbed his eyes. He saw nobody pulling Gumdrop
from above. So someone must be pushing him from below!
Swirly waves were breaking on the Loch and something like a tail
was sticking out. What...? Who...? Surely not...

Yes, it was the Loch Ness Monster herself! So the Monster was real
after all! Mr Oldcastle was astounded, but he remembered his
manners. 'Thank you very much indeed, Ma'am!' he stammered.

'Och, not at all!' replied
Mrs Nessie in her soft Scottish voice.
'We must not allow a beautiful
wee vehicle like this to rust in the water!'
Then she told him how worried she was about
tomorrow and all those photographers.
'I just cannot abide crowds and those
terrible flash cameras,' she said with a shudder.
Mr Oldcastle saw her point and decided to help her.

'I have a solution, Ma'am. If you would kindly get into Gumdrop I
will take you to a nearby Loch where you could safely stay until all
the fuss is over.'

Mrs Nessie was delighted to have a ride in Gumdrop. She squeezed herself in as best she could and they drove slowly along. Horace ran far behind Gumdrop to guard the Monster's tail.

Having settled her safely in the hideaway Loch, Mr Oldcastle drove back to Loch Ness in the morning. Near the Castle he was held up by the rude men from the lorry. They were all smiles now.
'The Monster will appear this morning, och aye?' said McBurp with a false Scottish accent. 'Spectators only £10!'

Mr Oldcastle growled and drove on. 'Photographers only £100!' grinned McLurk broadly. 'Full copyright included!' added McSneak.

But Mr Oldcastle drove past, muttering darkly.

The shore was crowded with photographers and reporters, on this last day of the Monster-hunting season. They had all paid heavily to see and photograph the Monster, and were waiting breathlessly for it to appear. Mr Oldcastle gazed out himself, wondering what could possibly emerge this time?

SEE THE
MONSTER
HERE!
TODAY

And there it was! The huge Monster plopped up from the deep like a cork, creating massive waves. As the cameras clicked and flashed, its immense tail swept across the shore in an arc, sending people head over heels. 'This is dangerous!' cried Mr Oldcastle as he drove Gumdrop swiftly to a safe distance.

But it was too late, and the Monster's tail banged
hard against the front wheel. Gumdrop gave
an angry HONK HONK and caught
the tail in the spokes of his wheel
and twisted it round, tight.
The result was terrible.

The Loch Ness Monster exploded!
In a blinding flash it flew apart
in a thousand pieces.
One piece landed near Professor
Whoppertaker who fell flat on his
back. He sat up and looked at it.

BANG!

'It's plastic!' he shouted. 'The Monster's a fake! There's never BEEN a real monster!!'

The others took up the cry and turned their cameras on Gumdrop, who had at last revealed the truth about the Monster. Mr Oldcastle was surrounded by reporters, but he didn't say a word about the real Mrs Nessie, safe in her hideaway Loch.

It was of course McBurp and his friends who did it. They were
London crooks called Burp and Lurk and Sneak, disguised as
improbable Scotsmen. Now that their plastic monster had
exploded, they took to their heels and drove away.
Little did they know that Horace
had been to their lorry meanwhile
and had quietly taken their bag
with all the money!
It was their fault – they should
not have kept their sausages
in the same bag!

Mr Oldcastle patted Horace for being such a clever boy and
gave the money back to the photographers.
And Horace ate the sausages.
Next morning there were headlines in all the papers:

Bang goes the Monster!

GUMDROP SLAYS MONSTER

VINTAGE CAR REVEALS HOAX!

MONSTER MYTH
EXPLODED: 'A FAKE'
SAYS PROFESSOR

MONSTER?
There is no such thing!

In smaller type each paper also carried the news that:

HORACE THE DOG RETRIEVES MONEY.

And every paper had a photograph of Gumdrop and Horace.

At last everybody had departed and Loch Ness was quiet again.
It was time to fetch Mrs Nessie back. She squeezed herself into
Gumdrop once more, and she wanted to do something
special for Mr Oldcastle in return.
'I am much obliged to you and your noble car,' she said.
'I see that you have a camera, mercifully without flash.
If you care to take a photograph, do meet me by the
Castle at midday tomorrow!'

Mr Oldcastle was absolutely delighted, and he drove Mrs Nessie carefully back to her own Loch again.

Next morning he drove
Gumdrop to the Castle in
good time and he was ready
with his camera.

Punctually at midday, out plopped Mrs Nessie with a smile.
And beside her, out plopped her husband Mr Monster himself,
and their five little monsters in a row!
And Mr Josiah Oldcastle took such a photograph as the
world had never seen before.

But he promised Mrs Nessie that he would never show it
to anyone. After all, the Loch Ness Monster had exploded
and there was no such thing!
So ever since that day, thanks to Gumdrop, Mrs Nessie
and her family can live in peace.